B is for Baby

An Alphabet of Verses

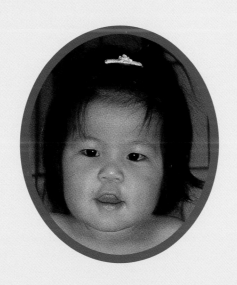

B is for Baby

An Alphabet of Verses

by MYRA COHN LIVINGSTON

photographs by STEEL STILLMAN

Margaret K. McElderry Books

Photos of the following babies were taken by Steel Stillman
with art direction and photo styling by Ann Bobco:
• Kelby Kamali Clark
• Maria Fredrica Mei-Yu Rinehart Jones
• Oliver Partridge Wade

Additional photos have been provided by the parents
of the following babies:
• Katherine Hale Apostolou • Bryan Robert Michael Benisvy
• Jack Ryan Benisvy • Jurriaan Elias Brugge • John Vincent D'Onofrio • Travis Jahnke
• Clio Testori Markman • David Harry Mele ("Ubiquitous" Babies) and
• Richard Gibbons Livingston ("Hiking" Baby)

Special thanks to all who participated in this book.

Margaret K. McElderry Books
An imprint of Simon & Schuster Children's Publishing Division
1230 Avenue of the Americas
New York, New York 10020
Text copyright © 1996 by Myra Cohn Livingston
Photographs copyright © 1996 by Steel Stillman
All rights reserved including the right of reproduction in whole or in part in any form.
Book design by Ann Bobco
The text of this book is set in Univers Extended
Printed in Hong Kong by South China Printing Co. (1988) Ltd.
First Edition
10 9 8 7 6 5 4 3 2 1

Library of Congress Cataloging-in-Publication Data
Livingston, Myra Cohn.
B is for baby : an alphabet of verses / Myra Cohn Livingston ; photographs by Steel Stillman—1st ed.
p. cm.
Summary: An alphabetized collection of poems about babies in all their moods and moments.
1. Infants—Juvenile poetry. 2. Children's poetry, American. 3. English language—Alphabet—Juvenile literature.
[1. Babies—Poetry. 2. American poetry. 3. Alphabet.] I. Stillman, Steel, ill. II. Title.
PS3562.I945B12 1996
8.11'.54—dc20
[E]
95-44784
CIP AC

ISBN 0-689-80950-6

For Richard Gibbons Livingston, Sally, and Josh
—M.L.

For Kate
—S.S.

A a

Awesome-Baby
came one day
in a newborn-baby way.

Baby's grandma,
old and wise,
said, "He has my mother's eyes!"

Baby's grandpa
gave a grin,
"But he has my father's chin!"

Baby
snuggled cosily,
happy simply just to be.

Bb

Bathtub-Baby
in the tub
likes his feet
to have a rub,

wants to feel
warm water squeeze
from his washcloth
to his knees.

Likes soap bubbles
caught in air,
pats white soapsuds
everywhere,

splashes water
anyplace,
likes to splatter
Mother's face,

wants to have
a little swim
with his mother
holding him—

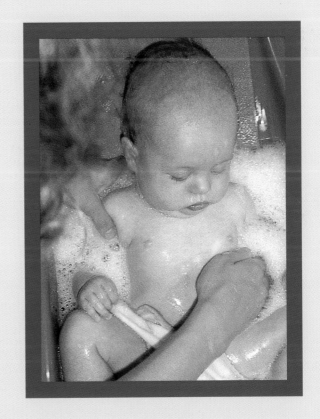

Cc

Christmas-Baby
wonders why
one small star
has climbed so high;
stares at golden balls
of light
like a hundred moons
of night;
watches
strands of tinsel
shine
silvery
through boughs of pine;
listening,
she turns to hear
Christmas carols
singing near;
falls asleep
and smiles to be
dreaming
of her Christmas tree.

Dd

What can Baby do but fret
when she finds herself all wet?

If she lets them know, then maybe
she can be Dry-Diaper-Baby.

Ee

Eating-Baby
cries:

Don't bother
ever
calling
to
my
father,

nor
my
sister
nor
my
brother.

Milk
comes
only
from
my
mother!

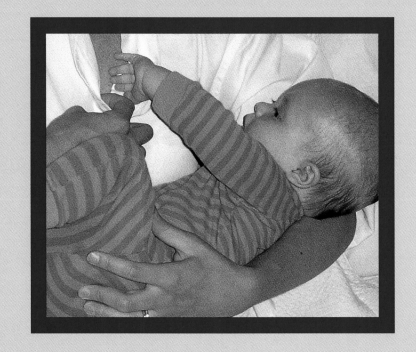

Ff

**Fussy-Baby
likes to fret.**

**Is he hungry?
Is he wet?**

**Fussy-Baby
looks at us:**

**Let me be,
I *like* to fuss!**

Gg

Gurgle-Baby
finds a note
somewhere
deep
within
her throat;

brings it up
and plays
around
giving it a
crowing
sound
like some
rare, exotic bird
nobody
has ever
heard;

but
her mother,
where she stands,
listens,
smiles,
and
understands!

Hiking-Baby's
in a pack,
jiggling on
his daddy's back,
up the path
and down the street,
hiking is
a weekend treat,
up the trail
and
down the road,
what a
joggly
little
load!

Ii

He doesn't
need
to drink or eat;

he's cozy,
warm
from hands to feet;

he has
his toys.
He has dry clothes;

and yet
he cries
of countless woes.

It simply
isn't
knowable

why
Baby's
inconsolable.

Jj

Jolly-Baby
sees the sun,
smiling as the day's begun,
glad to see
his mother's face,
glad to see
his special space,
glad to hear
his doggy bark,
glad he'll get to
see the park,
glad to find games
he can play,
glad when
morning comes
each day!

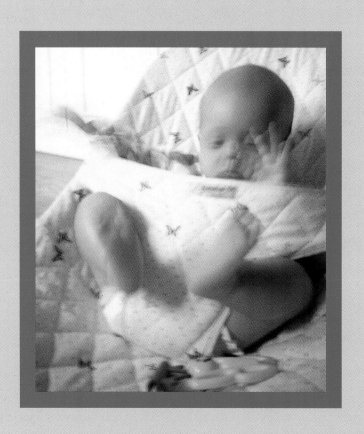

Kk

Kicking-Baby
tells his feet,
tells his toes
and tells his knees:

We'll kick
everything
we please—

kicking things
is really
neat!

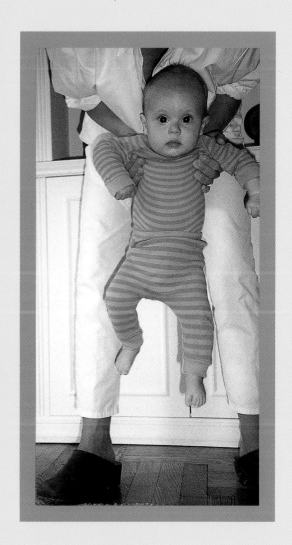

Ll

Little-Baby won't stay small.
Every day he grows.
It's a Law of Nature: *All
little babies don't stay small!*
Some grow sideways, some grow tall.
All outgrow their clothes.
Little-Baby won't stay small.
Every day he grows.

Mm

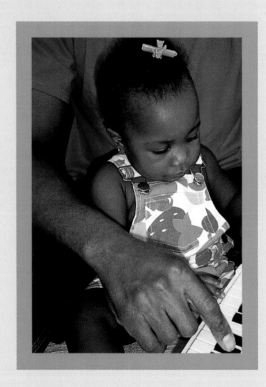

Music-Baby
hears a sound
when her mother
is around,
something
wonderful that floats
in a melody
of notes.

Music-Baby
understands:
When she sees her
father's hands
on the keyboard
there will rise
fascination—
and surprise.

Music-Baby
listens—hears
something happening
in her ears,
something deep
that she can never
name, but will know
forever—

N n

Nighttime-Baby
in his bed
folds one hand
above his head,
gives a little
baby hum,
feels his blanket,
sucks his thumb,
turns himself
from left to right,
settles down
into the night,
hidden
like a silent mouse,
in his little
blanket house—

Oo

Ogle-Baby thinks:

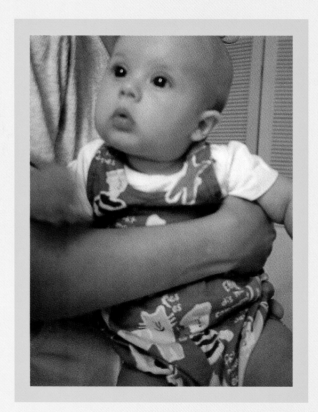

What's that
lying on the front door mat?

Why
do pictures hang on walls?

Who
makes shadows in the halls?

When
can we play in the park?

Where
do birds sing after dark?

How
do pages turn in books?

Ogle-baby blinks,

and looks!

Pulling-Baby
makes some passes;
tugs
on ears
and hair
and glasses—

Who wants rattles?
Who wants toys?

Pulling-Baby
just enjoys
grabbing
everything
she pleases,
tugging
everything
she seizes.

Most especially
she
needs

to
be
tugging
Mother's
beads.

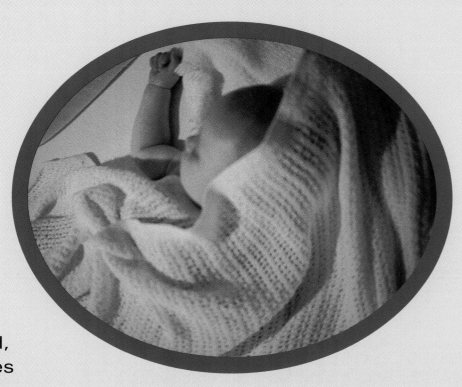

Qq

Quiet-Baby
in his bed,
toys asleep
and stories read,
watches pictures
on the wall,
flickering shadows
down the hall,
drowsing now with
half-closed eyes;
sleep will find him
where he lies,
dreaming in
another world
with his fingers
loosely curled.

Rr

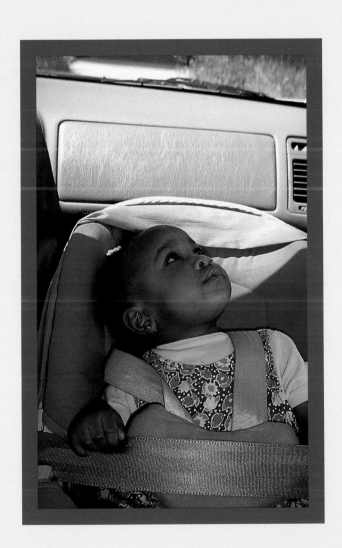

Riding-Baby
thinks it's neat
sitting in
her infant seat.

Off she goes
into the car,
one place near,
another far.

Out the window
she can see
house and sidewalk,
streetlight, tree,

She can watch
how all things near
soon grow small
and disappear.

What good fun
to spend the day
riding backward
all the way.

Swinging-Baby
loves to go
backward,
forward,
high
and
low

push her up
and then let go

swinging
to
and
swinging
fro

backward   forward

high
and
low

don't let go

to
and
fro

high
and
low

don't let
don't let
don't let

go

Tt

Throwing-Baby
likes her
toys

making
lots
and
lots
of
noise

when
she drops
them
on the floor.

Isn't that
what hands are for?

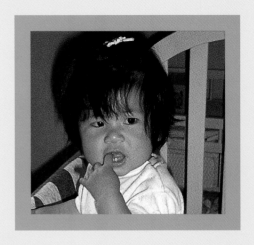

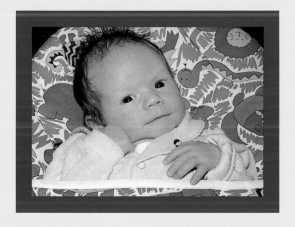

Uu

I can

tell you

only this:

Baby

is

U b i q u i t o u s !

V v

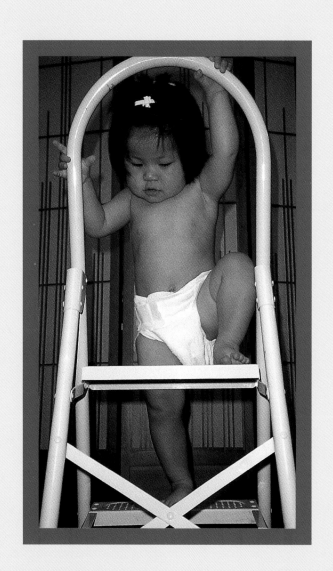

Now
her
fingers
grow
much
longer.

Now
her
muscles
feel
much
stronger.

Awesome
Baby's
growing
bigger,
burgeoning
with
Vim
and
Vigor!

Ww

Wriggle-Baby
starts
from
here

figures
how to
get to **near**

wants to go
some
otherwhere

twists
and squirms
and ends up
there

XXXX's

Her grandma gave her nose a kiss—
    she turned and squirmed away.
What silly thing, she thought, is this,
    to give a baby's nose a kiss?
    It's something foolish I can miss—
    today and every day!!
Her grandma gave her nose a kiss.
    She turned and squirmed away.

Yy

Little Baby,
very small,
doesn't make much noise
at all.

Older Baby,
by and by,
finds it helps a lot
to cry.

One thing's
easy to foretell:
Bigger Baby
learns to YELL—

Zz

All around
the living room
Daddy helps his
Baby zoom.

Like an airplane,
like a kite,
Superbaby
left and right

hums and buzzes
through the air,
Baby-Zooming
everywhere!